BEHIND THE SCENES BIOGRAPHIES

WHAT YOU NEVER KNEW ABOUT

TOM

HOLLAND

by Mari Bolte

CAPSTONE PRESS
a capstone imprint

This is an unauthorized biography.

Published by Spark, an imprint of Capstone
1710 Roe Crest Drive, North Mankato, Minnesota 56003
capstonepub.com

Copyright © 2025 by Capstone. All rights reserved. No part of this publication may be reproduced in whole or in part, or stored in a retrieval system, or transmitted in any form or by any means, electronic, mechanical, photocopying, recording, or otherwise, without written permission of the publisher.

Library of Congress Cataloging-in-Publication Data
Names: Bolte, Mari, author.
Title: What you never knew about Tom Holland / by Mari Bolte.
Description: North Mankato : Capstone Press, 2025. | Series: Behind the scenes biographies | Includes bibliographical references and index.
Audience: Ages 9-11 | Audience: Grades 4-6 Summary: "Tom Holland has danced across stages. He has swung across the big screen. But what is his life like behind the scenes? Does he do his own stunts? What are his fears? These questions and more will be answered in this high-interest, carefully leveled book that will enthrall reluctant and struggling readers"— Provided by publisher.
Identifiers: LCCN 2023047163 (print) | LCCN 2023047164 (ebook) | ISBN 9781669072911 (hardcover) | ISBN 9781669073147 (paperback) | ISBN 9781669072959 (pdf) | ISBN 9781669073154 (epub) | ISBN 9781669073161 (kindle edition)
Subjects: LCSH: Holland, Tom, 996—Juvenile literature. | Actors—Great Britain—Biography—Juvenile literature. | Dancers—Great Britain—Biography—Juvenile literature.
Classification: LCC PN2598.H58 B65 2025 (print) | LCC PN2598.H58 (ebook) | DDC 791.4302/8092 [B]—dc23/eng/20240122
LC record available at https://lccn.loc.gov/2023047163
LC ebook record available at https://lccn.loc.gov/2023047164

Editorial Credits
Editor: Christianne Jones; Designer: Elijah Blue; Media Researcher: Jo Miller; Production Specialist: Whitney Schaefer

Image Credits
Alamy: Album, 14, BFA, 8 (left), 16, Cinematic, 23 (top right), Entertainment Pictures, 23 (bottom left), Imaginechina Limited, 13, PA Images, 29, Storms Media Group, 9; Getty Images: Chung Sung-Jun, 4, Gabe Ginsberg, 5, Kevork Djansezian, 17, Alberto Alcocer, 20, Anthony Kwan, 26, Frazer Harrison, 8 (right), Gareth Cattermole, cover, Jose Perez/Bauer-Griffin, 19, Karwai Tang, 10, Kevin C. Cox, 7, Koki Nagahama, 27, Pablo Cuadra, 24; Shutterstock: Alona_S, 23 (bottom right), andriano.cz, 21 (left), Dauren Abildaev, 15, DFree, 11, Fred Duval, 21 (right), JosepPerianes, 12 (pen), lesyau_art, 18-19 (raindrops), Martial Red, 12 (pen stroke), 23 (top left), 25, okansurmen, 28, xpixel, 18-19

Design Elements: Shutterstock: IIIerlok_xolms

Any additional websites and resources referenced in this book are not maintained, authorized, or sponsored by Capstone. All product and company names are trademarks™ or registered® trademarks of their respective holders.

Printed in the United States   6191

TABLE OF CONTENTS

A Superhero Destiny 4

Tom True or Tom False 6

Spider-Man Spills the Beans 8

Fanatic Fans 12

Spider-Man's Super Skills 14

Famous Friends and Childhood Chums 20

Tom's Fantastic Firsts 22

Social Media Mindfulness 24

The Brothers Trust 26

Peter Barker 28

    Glossary 30

    Read More 31

    Internet Sites 31

    Index 32

    About the Author 32

Words in **bold** are in the glossary.

A SUPERHERO DESTINY

Tom Holland has always loved Spider-Man. Throughout his childhood, he had around 30 different Spider-Man costumes. He began swinging across the screen as Spider-Man in 2016.

So what don't you know about this amazing actor? It's time to find out!

TOM TRUE
OR TOM FALSE

1. Pizza is Tom's favorite food.

2. Tom is scared of spiders.

3. Tom has three older brothers.

4. Tom was the youngest actor to play Spider-Man.

5. Tom was born in October.

6. Tom has *dyslexia*.

7. Before becoming Spider-Man, Tom went to carpentry school.

8. Tom is obsessed with basketball.

1. FALSE (It's sushi.) **2.** TRUE **3.** FALSE (He has three younger brothers, Harry, Sam, and Paddy.) **4.** TRUE (He was just 20 years old.) **5.** FALSE (His birthday is June 1, 1996.) **6.** TRUE (He was diagnosed as a child.) **7.** TRUE **8.** FALSE (He's obsessed with golf.)

SPIDER-MAN
SPILLS THE BEANS

Tom is famous for spilling secrets. It's earned him the nickname "Spoiler-Man." He even spoiled the plot of *Jurassic World: Fallen Kingdom* for Marvel co-star Chris Pratt. Pratt hadn't even read the script yet!

Chris Pratt

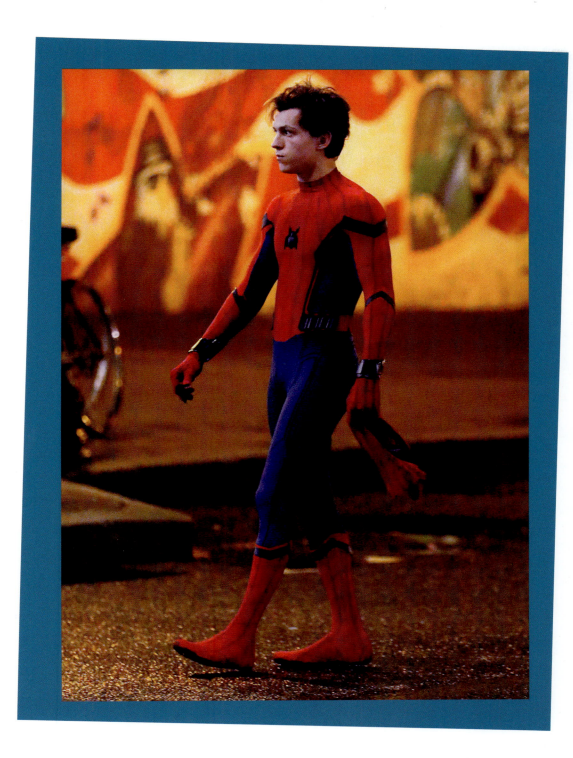

One well-known secret is Tom's relationship with Zendaya. They met in 2016. Soon after, they started showing up on each other's social media. For years, they insisted they were just friends. The pair went public as a couple in 2021.

Zendaya

FANATIC FANS

Sometimes fans get carried away. In 2019, Tom saved a fan in New York. She was getting crushed by people trying to get Tom's autograph. He calmed the crowd so they would move back. He made sure the fan was safe before signing more autographs.

SPIDER-MAN'S **SUPER** SKILLS

Dancing isn't just a hobby for Tom. He is a trained dancer. Around age 9, he started hip-hop classes. For two years, he trained in tap and ballet. At 12 years old, he starred in his first professional show. It was *Billy Elliot the Musical*.

FACT

Tom's dad was the one who took him to see *Billy Elliot the Musical* for the first time.

Tom took classes in **acrobatics** too. Those skills helped land him the role of Spider-Man. Tom performed as many **stunts** as possible in the Spider-Man movies.

Many celebrities perform on *Lip Sync Battle*. But Tom Holland set the standard. He went all out for his performance of "Umbrella" by Rihanna. There was even pouring rain during the dance!

". . . for all the movies that I'm incredibly proud of, the Lip Sync Battle *is what I get the most compliments for."*
—Tom Holland

FAMOUS FRIENDS AND CHILDHOOD CHUMS

Chris Hemsworth

Tom is close to his Marvel co-stars. His famous friends include Robert Downey Jr., Chris Hemsworth, and Jake Gyllenhaal. But his best friend is Harrison Osterfield. They've known each other since they were teens.

Harrison Osterfield

FACT
Tom and Harrison met at the BRIT School. It's a British performing arts school in England.

Tom's Fantastic FIRSTS

It took Tom eight **auditions** to land his role in *Billy Elliot the Musical*. However, he has had a lot of incredible firsts.

FIRST Professional Theater Performance
Billy Elliot the Musical

FIRST Feature Film
The Impossible

FIRST Appearance as Spider-Man
Captain America: Civil War

FACT
Tom's first tattoo was a Spider-Man symbol. It's on the bottom of his foot.

SOCIAL MEDIA MINDFULNESS

In 2022, Tom took a **social media** break. He was working on a movie called *The Crowded Room*. It was a very emotional role. It took a **toll** on him. He needed to focus on his **mental health**.

Tom supports the stem4 **charity**. It shines a light on positive mental health in teenagers. He encouraged his followers to support stem4 when he announced his social media break.

THE BROTHERS
TRUST

Tom's family has a charity called The Brothers Trust. His parents started it in 2017. Tom and his brothers run it. The Brothers Trust supports other charities. It raises money for causes that aren't always heard.

PETER BARKER

Tom loves dogs. He has rescued several, including two of his own dogs. Their names are Tessa and Pistachio. In 2019, Tom helped find homes for rescue dogs. One of the dogs was named Peter Barker. Its superhero name was Dog-Dog.

Glossary

audition (aw-DIH-shuhn)—a tryout performance

charity (CHAR-uh-tee)—an organization that helps those in need

dyslexia (dis-LEK-see-uh)—a learning disability usually marked by problems in reading, spelling, and writing

mental health (MEN-tuhl HELTH)—how we think, feel, and behave

social media (SOH-shuhl MEE-dee-uh)—the way people share information through technology

stunt (STUHNT)—a trick or feat that shows great skill

toll (TOHL)—something that causes damage or suffering

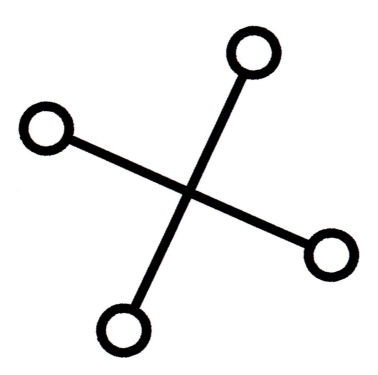

Read More

Borgert-Spaniol, Megan. *Tom Holland: Acting Superstar*. Minneapolis: Big Buddy Books, 2022.

Gardiner, Nora. *Tom Holland*. New York: Enslow Publishing, 2022.

Kawa, Katie. *Tom Holland: Making a Difference as a Movie Star*. Buffalo, NY: KidHaven Publishing, 2024.

Internet Sites

Britannica Kids: Spider-Man
kids.britannica.com/students/article/Spider-Man/606595

The Brothers Trust
thebrotherstrust.org

Marvel Universe for Young Readers
marvel.com/comics/discover/140/marvel-universe-for-young-readers

Index

acrobatics, 16
auditions, 22

Billy Elliott the Musical, 15
birthday, 7
brothers, 6, 7, 27

charity work, 25, 27

dancing, 15
dogs, 28, 29

family, 6, 7, 15, 27
favorite food, 6
friends, 10, 21

Lip Sync Battle, 18

mental health, 25
movies, 18
   Captain America: Civil War, 22
   Crowded Room, The, 25
   Impossible, The, 22
   Jurassic World: Fallen Kingdom, 8
   Spider-Man franchise, 6, 16

nickname, 8

relationships, 10

school, 6, 21
social media, 10, 25
stunts, 16

tattoo, 23

About the Author

Mari Bolte is the author and editor of hundreds of children's books. Every book is her favorite book as long as the readers learned something and enjoyed themselves!